Edgar Graduates

written by **Dr. Mary Ann Shallcross Smith**
illustrated by **Rebecca Compton**

Thank you to
Alicia, Amy, Aria, Danielle, Duffy, Eleanor,
Ellie, Eric, Kathryn, Kenny, Lisa, Ron,
Stefanie, Tim, and Tracy
for your support, guidance and insight.

Additionally, my sincerest gratitude to
Keith for reading this book to his sons Mitchell, Benjamin, and Oliver,
Christopher for reading this book to his daughter Alta,
and Andrew for reading this book to his daughter Avery.

Thank you for giving me valuable feedback from a young reader's
perspective and for including my grandchildren in the creation of this book.

This book belongs to:

_____

My Graduations:

_____

_____

_____

_____

_____

_____

Hi! I'm Edgar.

I am graduating preschool today!

I remember when I first started school...

I started school when I was just a baby.

6

When I was an infant, I slept a lot!

I also learned to smile, roll over, sit up, crawl, walk, and even how to say a few words.

I used to wear diapers.

Not any more! Now I am potty trained.

When I was a toddler, I couldn't write my name.
But I did learn my ABCs!

In preschool, I took my naps on a cot.
No more naps after graduation!

After my preschool graduation, I will graduate from kindergarten and I will graduate from elementary school. Then I will graduate from middle school.

Before you know it, I will be going to high school!

Gg   Hh   Ii   Ll   Mm

When I'm in high school,
I will be a freshman my first year.
I will be a sophomore my second year.
I will be a junior my third year.
I will be a senior my fourth year.

Then I will graduate from high school!

19

After I graduate high school, I will have lots of choices.
I can choose to go to a college or take classes online.
I can choose to go to a technical school.
I can choose to join the military.
I can choose to volunteer or find a place to work.

I can choose from so many different things!

Diploma

Edgar is hereby awarded this degree and is now a graduate!

However, before I can receive my Associate's Degree, Bachelor's Degree, Master's Degree, or Doctorate Degree, today I am going to graduate from preschool with my friends!

I will walk across the stage to the tune of "Pomp and Circumstance."
I will wear a cap and gown – my cap even has a tassel!

My family, friends, and teachers will be so proud of me.
I am proud of me!

I will receive a diploma with my name on it!

This means I am now a graduate!

This is the first of many graduations
I will achieve!

Can you find these words?

Associate's Degree

Bachelor's Degree

college

diploma

Doctorate Degree

freshman

high school

junior

Master's Degree

middle school

military

senior

sophomore

tassel

technical school

Go back in the story to find them!

What do these words mean? Turn the page to find out!

# Definitions:

Associate's Degree: an academic degree awarded by a community college, junior college, technical college, or a bachelor's degree-granting college or university, after completing 2 years of school

Bachelor's Degree: an academic degree awarded by a college or university, after completing 4 years of school

college (or university): an institution of higher learning

diploma: a certificate given after completing school

Doctorate Degree: the highest level of academic or professional degrees

freshman: a student in the first year of university, college, or high school

high school: school attended after elementary school, middle school, or junior high school

junior: a student in the third year of university, college, or high school

Master's Degree: a degree awarded by a graduate school

middle school: a school between elementary school and high school

military: a force that defends a country and its citizens

senior: a student in the fourth year of university, college, or high school

sophomore: a student in the second year of university, college, or high school

tassel: cords strung together and attached to a graduation cap

technical school: a two-year college that provides mostly employment skills for trained labor

Thank you to:

Ebenezer, age 1. Ebenezer lives in North Providence, RI.

Elizabeth, age 5. Elizabeth lives in North Providence, RI.

Konnor Aponte, age 1. Konnor lives in Lincoln, RI.

Ava Barlow, age 8. Ava lives in North Providence, RI.

Bryce and Ethan Bartlett, age 5. Bryce and Ethan live in Smithfield.

Yazhara Burleigh, age 3.

Ian Ciffo, age 3. Ian lives in Warwick, RI.

James Delbarone, age 4. James lives in West Warwick, RI.

Preston Demello, age 8. Preston lives in Foster, RI.

Zoey Dempsy, age 3. Zoey lives in Chepachet, RI.

Juakeem Dennis. age 2. Juakeem lives in Pawtucket, RI.

McKenzie Gierhart, age 4.

Adriana Houle, age 6.

Willow Johnson, age 3.

Christian, Faith, and Journey Joly, ages 4, 5, and 2.

Lance Lassiter, age 4. Lance lives in Pascoag, RI.

Diem Mutter, age 2. Diem lives in Cumberland, RI.

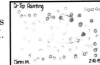

Nicholas Ortiz, age 3.

Isaac Paradis, age 11 months. Isaac lives in Burrillville, RI.

Kori Peters, age 9. Kori lives in Foster, RI.

Alyssa Powell, age 3. Alyssa lives in Woonsocket, RI.

Ziva Provost, age 4. Ziva lives in Lincoln, RI.

Alta Smith, age 1. Alta lives in Smithfield, RI.

Madeline Smith, age 2. Madeline lives in East Greenwich, RI.

Alaniis Tavares, age 4. Alaniis lives in Pawtucket, RI.

Avery Vogel, age 4. Avery lives in Cumberland, RI.

Dr. Mary Ann Shallcross Smith

Dr. Mary Ann Shallcross Smith lives in Rhode Island and is known to most as "Dr. Day Care." She has proved herself to be an expert in the field and received her Doctorate in Education and Leadership. She has been an early childhood professional for over 40 years, starting her home-based child care when her son Keith was born. Over her professional career, she has owned 28 child care facilities.

A late bloomer in her personal educational journey, Mary Ann returned to school 10 years after graduating from Lincoln High School. Despite growing up in a time when her family did not value higher education, she continued to pursue her education until she received her Doctorate degree.

Through her work, Dr. Shallcross Smith realized that families need to bring educational words into their homes to make education more achievable and part of the family conversation. By valuing and talking about the possibility of continued education, it becomes more attainable for all children. Education is so important – it opens the door to many possibilities. Mary Ann hopes that this book will help families have conversations about educational options. The idea for this story is something that Mary Ann has dreamed of for many years, and she appreciates the support that made this book a reality.

Mary Ann Shallcross Smith is married to Ron Smith. Her adult children are Keith Shallcross, Chris Smith, and Amy Vogel. They make her life exceptional!

Rebecca Compton

Rebecca Compton is from Pennsylvania and currently lives in Rhode Island. She has her Bachelor's Degree in Early Childhood Education and Elementary Education from Juniata College. While working with early childhood and elementary school children for over ten years, she has always enjoyed sharing her love of art and books with children and always hoped to illustrate her own children's book. After she created the Dr. Day Care Learning Center mascot Edgar nearly two years ago, illustrating a book about him has been a goal for both Mary Ann and Rebecca.

Made in the USA
Middletown, DE
21 May 2015